THIS HAWK BELONGS TO ME

written and illustrated by
JO POLSENO

DAVID McKAY COMPANY, INC.
NEW YORK

Library of Congress Cataloging in Publication Data

Polseno, Jo.
This hawk belongs to me.

SUMMARY: An eleven-year-old boy in New York
City finds a dying baby kestrel in the marshes of
Long Island, restores it to health, and tries to
prepare it to return to its own environment.
1. Kestrels—Legends and stories. [1. Kestrels
—Fiction. 2. Falcons—Fiction] I. Title.
PZ10.3.P444Th   [Fic]   76-12745
ISBN 0-679-20324-9

MANUFACTURED IN THE UNITED STATES OF AMERICA

jP 764th

Dedicated to
my mother,
who tolerated my strange
collection of turtles and
toads, bugs and birds, and
whatever else I could drag in
from the forests and fields

Walk down Lexington Avenue around five o'clock on any afternoon and listen to the noise—the laughter and the screams from the kids playing in the street. Listen to the vegetable vendors haggle, argue and throw up their hands in mock disgust. See the cheese and salami hanging in the windows and the barrels of black olives blocking the doorway of the grocery stores. You can still hear Russ Columbo and Enrico Caruso singing Italian love songs that drift out from the tenement windows. Sweet basil grows on the windowsills and tomato plants grow in five-gallon cans.

Almost everyone in this Italian neighborhood is related. Everybody knows everybody else's business. Take, for instance, Dino De Angelo. He's not in school today and everybody knows it already except, of course, his mother, Antonia De Angelo. She is in the kitchen rolling out homemade pasta. Dino's sister, Raphaella, has come home for lunch and is just informing her weary mother that Dino has disappeared from school again.

"*Mamma mia!*" wailed Antonia. "He's gonna grow up dumb, just like his Uncle Pasquale."

Actually, Dino is a self-educated truant. At the moment, there are any number of places where he might be found. He might be in the dark and dismal Wood Duck Pond or a place called the Cascades. Either way he is out discovering things for himself. Once he discovered a horses' graveyard. There were bleached bones lying all around this spooky meadow. It reminded Dino of the elephants' graveyard in a Tarzan movie. Now most of the horses' skulls are down in his cellar. He sold a few skulls, but squeamish parents made their kids return them. Of course, Dino kept the money.

Once he found an underground cavern, full of water, that disappeared into the side of a hill and went on forever. His kid brother, Luigi, almost drowned when his inner tube sprang a leak after striking a sharp rock. Dino convinced Luigi that there were giant teeth marks on the tube and that he had barely escaped being devoured by a monster that ate only tender seven-year-old Italians.

However, today the place that Dino is NOT is St. Augustine's school. He is down by the sea, where the tall grasses grow. He is with Dom Dinardo, his nineteenth cousin. (Now that's really Italian.) Dominick, like Dino, had an upset stomach from something he didn't eat and got excused from classes by the school nurse. Mrs. Adams is not only very nice, she is also very gullible, and Dino and Dom are very good actors. They got all of their training at home.

At the moment, they are deep in the marshes near Fairfield Beach, somewhere in the grass way over their heads, about to

make another discovery.... They're lost! They are not, however,
too bothered by that possibility.

They are thrashing blindly about in the high-tufted reeds—
two eleven-year-olds sounding more like eleven two-year-olds.
One of them, Dino, has black, curly hair and a nose that is kind
of big for his age. Dominick has straight hair, with a fake wave
in it, and wears glasses as thick as the bottom of a Coke bottle.
His glasses are always hanging off the end of his nose. Dino's
hair is always hanging over his eyes. Between them they sure
could use one good "seeing-eye" friend.

They could be hanging around the corner like most of the kids on their city block. But no, they're out there in the wilds, searching for the answers to at least two questions: Are they really hopelessly lost? And did the school nurse call home?

Anyway, imagine them in the soft, brown marshes of Fairfield, one bus ride in the opposite direction from school. The things they are learning they would never learn from Sister Mary Monica, such as how mean and aggressive nesting red-winged blackbirds can be, how hard blue crabs can bite or how gracefully a marsh hawk can fly.

If Dino and Dom can hang in there for another hour or so, there is a good chance that they will stagger their way through the grass, fall flat on their faces with fear and exhaustion, and discover, for the rest of the truants on their city block, Long Island Sound.

At this point their conversation is tense with the realization of their desperate situation.

"You can't make me believe that a nine-year-old kid wears a toupee!" shouts Dominick.

"He had scarlet fever and all his hair fell out," lies Dino.

Already you can see how serious these kids are about discovering Long Island Sound.

They are talking about Ronald McDonald, the kid from the Irish neighborhood. Ronnie shows every sign of being a writer or a great poet by the time he reaches the seventh grade—that is, if he ever reaches the seventh. He's been in the "dummy" sixth for two years in a row, mostly because of playing hooky, the true chronic disease of both neighborhoods. Ronnie doesn't wear fake hair at all. His hair is just blond and bushy, and Dino, as usual, just made it up—about the toupee, that is.

Dom and Dino are knee-deep in muck and the going is getting rougher and tougher. In fact, Dino's stomach is *really* beginning to hurt.

"Dom! Look over there! A dead tree! Maybe we can climb it and see which way is out of here."

"We'll never get out of here and it's all your fault again, Dino."

"All my fault, all my fault! That's all I ever hear when things get rough! What about the haunted house with all those stuffed birds we found?" yelled Dino excitedly. Which actually sounded like "AllmyfaultallmyfaultthatsallIeverhearwhenthingsgetrough . . . etc."

That's how fast and loud neighborhood kids talk when they get excited, which is most of the time; but with the help of all those hand signals, they seem to understand each other rather well. Communicating is no problem.

(By the way, Dom fell through the floor of that spooky house and landed in the cellar. He was trying to make off with a suit of armor. It must have weighed a ton. The hole in the floor is still there and so is the armor.) At this moment Dominick was stuck in the mud and could not move.

Dino managed to get unstuck and reach the base of the dead

tree. Near the top was a large black hole—something to hang on to, he thought. He tried desperately to pull his feet out of the muck and climb the crooked tree, but just as he got one foot free he saw two beautiful dead birds lying in the reeds.

"Hey, Dom! Look what I've found!" Dead things do not bother true explorers.

Dom struggled over, picked up one of them and cried, "It looks like one of the stuffed birds we found in that haunted house."

Dino brushed the hair from his eyes and noticed how beautifully the birds were marked.

What they had found was a pair of dead kestrels, the smallest and the most handsome type of falcon in North America.

"Somebody must have shot them," exclaimed Dino.

"Do you think we can get anything for them?" asked Dominick scientifically.

"I dunno. Maybe that old guy in Fairfield who stuffs birds for the museum will give us a buck apiece—that is, if we ever get out of here alive! I'd better climb the tree; it's getting dark."

It was an easy tree to climb, even with muddy sneakers. Nearing the top, Dino could hear an old truck clanking down a dirt road. It didn't sound too far off. They were not *that* lost, after all.

"There's a whole ocean out there," shouted Dino, "and the road is only fifty yards away." His hand was on the edge of the hole when something bit it!

"Ouch! *Mamma mia*! There's something alive in that hole!"

Rays from the evening sun were slanted so that Dino could see into the cavity—enough to see that whatever it was wasn't very large. He stuck his hand into the hole and came up with a frightened, angry, screeching, fluffy kestrel hawklet.

Not only had Dino and Dom discovered Long Island Sound for the kids on the corner, but Dino had found an orphan that would change his summer and perhaps more than that.

It was already agreed that *if* they saw car lights, Dominick would fall down and play "heart attack" and Dino would go into some wild Italian double-talk about getting the kid a priest or getting him to a hospital.

"I just changed my mind," said Dominick. "There might be snakes in that grass. If a car stops, I'll tell them you got no arms."

"O.K. Knock it off, Dom. We gotta walk and that's all there is to it, so let's go."

Grimly, the two explorers decided to do the scout pace—walk

fifty yards and run fifty yards. It was two hours before the boys reached the Post Road. The buses had stopped running. Sometime after midnight, a sweet little old lady stopped to see what was wrong with that little boy lying by the side of the road. She really believed Dominick was having a heart attack and that Dino had no arms.

It was three o'clock in the morning before they finally got home. There was a police car parked in front of Dino's tenement. Dominick took one look and disappeared down the street without even saying good-bye.

****

"But, Mom, why a thirteen-state alarm when I was only nine hours late?" asked Dino after the police had left.

"Because I thought you ran away from home again like when you were four years old," she said as she warmed up the leftover spaghetti. Antonia was upset but more relieved that this crazy kid of hers was back home—and safe.

Dino was busy filling a soup bowl with shredded newspaper, making a temporary nest for the hawk. When Antonia turned to fill his plate, she was too weary to complain. After all, a kid who would take nine ducklings to bed every night and kneel down to eat leftovers with his dog had to be a little weird. Antonia's biggest problem was trying to understand him. "It's got to come from his father's side, not mine," she said to herself.

"I suppose you're going to take him to bed with you?"

"Of course! As soon as I feed him some spaghetti."

Dino was going to have trouble with *this* bird. He had yet to learn that hawks are meat-eaters, and the fluffy, little bird nesting in the soup bowl was very close to death.

****

The next morning Dino awoke in a panic. The tiny bird next to his pillow was hardly breathing. He quickly dressed and ran into the kitchen. It was Saturday morning, so there was no hassle about school. His sister was at the breakfast table.

"Squeal-cat," he muttered. Then he said, "Mom, I gotta call Mr. Novak. I think the bird is almost dead."

"You can't. The phone has been turned off . . . again."

It seemed that something was always being turned off—or taken away by bill collectors—ever since his father had died.

There was no time to lose. Dino put the hawk in a shoe box and headed for Fairfield Avenue to "thumb" a ride.

Dino preferred to hitch rides at signal lights. That was where his acting ability and Latin charm were at their best. If there was time between light changes, he would ask the drivers if they wanted their windshields washed or if maybe he could check their oil. It worked most of the time, but today was the day that a ride meant life or death for the pitiful little creature in the Thom McAn shoe box.

His hastily made-up prayers were quickly answered. The driver of the first car to stop at the light was a nice man who looked like St. Francis of Assisi. He drove the desperate boy directly to the bird sanctuary, where Mr. Novak was curator. "Curator" was a word Dino would definitely have to look up in the dictionary someday.

It started to drizzle. The day was dreary enough to begin with. St. Francis (as Dino had dubbed his driver) pulled into the gravel driveway. The scratching in the shoe box had stopped. Dino was afraid to open the lid.

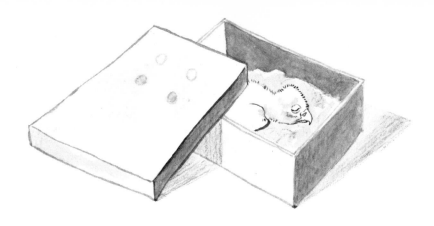

****

Mr. Novak carefully lifted the fragile creature from the box. There was very little life left in the bird.

"I'm sorry, Dino. I don't think there is much of a chance for this bird to survive. There isn't any food in his crop and it doesn't appear as though he's been fed for days. Where did you find him?"

Dino told him the whole story. Mr. Novak went into the house and returned with bits of hamburger and a pair of eyebrow tweezers.

"You see, Dino? The fact that a kestrel is not gasping for air is a good sign. If we can force-feed him some meat, there might be a chance to save him."

"Do kestrels eat spaghetti?" asked Dino.

Mr. Novak laughed. "No, they don't. Kestrels are birds of prey. That means they eat fresh meat, things like mice or rats, and sometimes songbirds—bones, feathers and all."

"Mice and rats he can catch in my kitchen, but there isn't a songbird within five miles of my house."

When Mr. Novak approached the bird with the meat, the fledgling quivered and opened his hungry mouth. With rapid, very-much-alive movements he almost ate the tweezers. Mr. Novak smiled and Dino could hardly believe his eyes. The starving bird ate until his crop was blown up like a balloon.

"He's going to *bust* any minute if you don't stop feeding him," yelled the frightened, happy Dino.

The curator laughed and explained to the concerned boy that nature also provided a safety valve for most birds. When its crop gets full, the bird can no longer open its beak.

Slowly, the drizzle stopped and the sun shone through the gray sky. The wet green grass glistened and the warmth of the sun brought forth the sweet smell of honeysuckle–it brought forth, too, the hope that this scrawny orphan was going to live.

Now, thought Dino, I can start thinking of a name for this bird because this hawk belongs to me!

✳✳✳✳✳✳✳✳✳✳✳

Mr. Novak "lent" Dino enough money to get home by bus. Instead, Dino bought twenty-five cents' worth of hamburger for the bird and a Hershey bar for himself. The panic over, he was in no great hurry to get home, so he sat on the freshly mown lawn of the Fairfield town green and gazed in wonder and relief at his sleeping beauty. He stroked the fluffy down and touched the bird's sharp blue beak. Its legs were bright yellow, ending with little black claws that were ever so sharp—ever so small. The bird slept all the way home even though the teen-ager who gave Dino a ride was a madman at the wheel.

As soon as the boy and his hawk got home, Dino made a nest from a packing box and filled it with straw and shredded newspaper. He made plans to go back to the marsh and look for the kestrel's dead parents. He also would have to work out a balanced diet for the bird—whatever that meant!

Chopped meat would do fine for a while, but as the hawk grew, it would need mice and rats. Mr. Novak said chicken heads would be fine—brains, feathers and all. Maybe that's a "balanced diet," thought Dino.

Dino decided to take his hawk down to the corner and show it to the kids. Everything was the same—cars screeching and kids screaming. The neighborhood kids were playing stickball and the storekeepers were yelling about losing business and who was going to pay for the broken windows.

"Hey, Dino! Dinardo said you found an ocean!" yelled Tony Esposito.

"Yeah, and look what else!" exclaimed Dino as the kids crowded around the shoe box.

The gang was not very impressed. They thought the hawk was a leftover Easter chick with a swollen nose, or a bedroom slipper with a blue beak.

"It's a baby eagle," said Dino. They wouldn't know the difference anyway.

Dominick was waiting on Dino's porch. Dino spoke. "Tomorrow morning I'm going back to the swamp to look for those dead birds. Wanna come? If they're still there, Mr. Novak will mount them and put them in a showcase. They're worth a buck apiece if they haven't started to rot."

Dominick agreed on one condition—that he would *not* hitchhike. He would go only if Dino got up the bus fare—*both ways*. Dino said he would get the money somehow as soon as he fed his orphan. He'd sell his father's army canteen or maybe his kid brother's shoes.

* * * * * * * * * * *

Sunday morning, Dino's conscience got the best of him. After all, his brother had only one pair of shoes and there was a bullet hole in his father's canteen, so it wouldn't hold any water. Missing Mass was bad enough. How many sins can an eleven-year-old kid handle, anyway?

At six in the morning, Dominick was still fast asleep. Dino rapped on the cracked windowpane until another piece of glass fell off. When he got no response, he clambered back down the rickety fire escape and headed for the marshes alone. It was still too early in the morning for the buses to start operating, and since he didn't have any money, he might as well go down to the Post Road and hope for a friendly delivery truck driver to have pity on him.

It was so early in the morning that a bakery truck actually stopped and the driver checked to see if the kid lying on the side of the road was all right. It was Sunday, so Dino told the truth. He was dying from starvation. After smelling the freshly baked bread, he offered to buy a loaf with money he didn't have. The young driver told him to forget it and gave him a loaf for free. The sun was touching the tips of the telephone poles when the truck stopped at the road that led to the marsh.

****

In the morning light Dino saw all the things that he and Dominick had missed in the dark. The silent emptiness of the night of the lonely marsh was filled now with golden shafts of sunlight. The tufted reeds that grew by the side of the road were shaken and gracefully bent by blackbirds and grackles perched on their fluffy tips.

Long-billed marsh wrens chattered in the grass and dozens of strange birds exploded from the marsh as the boy walked in wonderment down the road that would end at the sea.

Dino scattered bits of his loaf of bread to the wind and was delighted to see the blackbirds flit from the reeds to accept his offering. Herring gulls joined the blackbirds and the boy heard

for the first time the wild sounds that come from the throats of
the seabirds.

The gulls hovered over his head and he tossed more bread
crumbs into the air. The gigantic birds swooped down from the
sky and caught the morsels before they hit the ground.

"Now it's my turn to eat," yelled Dino as he sat down by the
side of the road to eat what was left of the bread. Screams of
protest came from the gulls.

When the bread was gone, the sky was empty. His fickle
feathered friends had departed.

Dino rose to his feet and decided to run the rest of the way.
The steady pounding of the silent surf was another strange
sound to him. He had *heard* it, in the dark, two nights before.
In a moment he would actually *see* an ocean.

****

Mr. Novak felt badly that someone would shoot the kestrels during the nesting season; however, they were in spring plumage and would make excellent mounted specimens. He gave Dino two dollars for the birds and the boy returned the money he had borrowed. After all, it was still Sunday!

While Mr. Novak was making change, Dino heard a strange-sounding cry coming from the towering tulip tree that grew next to the workshop.

"What's that?" asked the excited boy.

The sound came again. "KLEE ... KLEE ... KLEE ... KLEE ... KLEE ... KLEE." It had a wild, marshland sound, with all the ferocity the boy had heard from the angry gulls.

"That, my boy, is the hunting call of a kestrel," said Mr. Novak.

"It sounded like 'Kelly, Kelly, Kelly' to me," exclaimed Dino. "I think I'll call my little hawk Kelly. Yeah! That's what I'll call him—Kelly! How does that sound, Mr. Novak? I'll even baptize him—Kelly Anunzio De Angelo."

The curator laughed, handed the boy his change and said he must get to work skinning the birds immediately. This time, Dino would really take the bus, for he must hurry home to feed Kelly Anunzio De Angelo.

Goldberg's Kosher Meat Market was a couple of blocks from Dino's neighborhood. Every Friday morning there would be fresh chickens hanging from the iron hooks in the window, chickens with no heads. Dino was thinking to himself that those heads had to be somewhere. So he asked.

"What do you do with your chicken heads, Mr. Goldberg?" asked Dino, standing in the sawdust.

"With my *what?*"

"Those chickens in the window; they've got no heads. I wanna buy a couple. Only their heads!"

Mr. Goldberg turned to a customer. "A nickel I can't make on a chicken's head. Well, maybe a nickel, but that's all!" Without looking at Dino, he said, "In the backroom. Help yourself. Two heads for a nickel. Abe will tell you where to find them." Then in his most saccharine manner, "May I help you, Mrs. Silverman?"

Dino disappeared through the swinging door.

"That poor child," whispered Mrs. Silverman. "Things have got to be pretty bad when people have to live on chicken heads. The kid's not Jewish, is he?"

"No, Mrs. Silverman. I think he's from the Italian neighborhood. If he's really poor, I'll throw in a few wings and necks. Still makes pretty decent chicken soup, you know. Now, what can I do for you?"

"That kid's going to haunt me, Mr. Goldberg. Chicken heads? Chicken heads, two for a nickel? A bargain it is, but how long can anybody live on chicken heads? Wrap up a small fryer and put it on my bill. I won't be able to sleep tonight. He looks a *little* Jewish to me."

Dino wasn't too surprised when the butcher wrapped six chicken heads and one fryer for only fifteen cents, for Dino had

GOLDBERG'S

a wisdom far beyond his years. Mr. Goldberg told Dino to thank the kind lady.

"A chicken with six heads? My mother will never believe it, but it will keep her alive a few more days," smiled Dino, as he feigned shyness by making an arc in the sawdust with the toe of his shoe, all the while watching the tears develop in Mrs. Silverman's eyes.

"Now get out of here," said Mr. Goldberg, wiping his nose on his leather cuffs.

"Thank you both very much," called Dino as he returned to the noisy, bustling sidewalk. Kelly Anunzio would eat well tonight and so would the rest of the De Angelos, but would his mother believe that a plucked chicken got hit by a car?

Kelly was of the smallest species of hawks, and to survive the wilds he had to be tough—as tough as Cherry Nose Scalzo, the toughest kid on the block. Dino figured that the worst thing he could do to this bird would be to make him into a pet. He had to keep Kelly wild and fierce so that when he returned him to the Fairfield marshes he would still be able to survive—to fend for himself, even though his middle name was Anunzio.

****

The weeks passed by. Dino stopped playing hooky. Why shouldn't he? The school year was almost over. The hawk grew larger. It started to get spots and speckles, and the downy fluff had almost disappeared. Kelly left the bushel basket more often and scampered around the room. He perched on the curtain rods and peered inquisitively out the window.

His voice changed from a nervous squeak to a shrill screech. He grew wing feathers that were rusty brown and bluish black. There was an encasement around the base of each wing feather. Mr. Novak told Dino that when the feathers broke through the encasements, the hawk would be able to fly.

Once in a while Kelly would see a mouse scoot across the room; but since he didn't have to hunt for his food, he paid little or no attention. More often, Kelly would perch on the curtain rod and flap his wings at a tremendous rate of speed, as if he knew his wings could carry him away, but he wasn't quite sure. Someday, he's going to up and fly right out that window, thought Dino.

****

Uncle Pasquale sat at the kitchen table, drinking a glass of homemade wine. He was Antonia's brother and lived three houses down the street from Dino. He had just come down from the roof, where he had fed his pigeons. He never talked much, but when you have a face that looks like a clenched fist, who needs to talk?

"Did you start your garden yet?" asked Antonia.

"Si, pommadorros and *pubadules,"* he mumbled.

"Only tomatoes and peppers? How come?"

"Because I don't havva the time and I don't gotta the space."

"Dino could take care of your pigeons. You know how good he is with birds," said Antonia.

"Listen to me, Antonia. Dino doesn't have to take care of the pigeons. That hawk he's raising will take care of the pigeons. Remember, back in the old country, what the hawks did? They used to fly into the coop, kill the pigeons and only eat the heads. Remember, Antonia?"

Dino's mother tried to explain to Pasquale that the falcons of Italy came from North Africa and that they were larger and more ferocious than Kelly.

"Why, Kelly Anunzio is only as big as a robin. Come on. I'll show you how small he is," she said.

She opened the door to Dino's room. The window was open and the hawk was gone.

****

Dino was playing stickball. He was at bat when something swooped down from the sky and landed on his head.

"Dino, don't kill it. It's Kelly Anunzio!" shouted Dom Dinardo.

Dino fell to the ground laughing as the rest of the kids gathered around in disbelief. Dino himself could hardly believe that Kelly had learned to fly and that the bird had not flown away from home for good.

Kelly hopped from Dino's head to the sawed-off broom handle the boy used for a bat. Kelly had something in his claws. It was a gray city mouse, but Kelly acted as though he didn't know what to do with it! He had proved he could catch a mouse, but he did not yet associate it with food. And since a chicken's head didn't run about unless it was attached to a chicken's body, Kelly was going to be in for some confusing moments.

In fact, Kelly was afraid of the mouse and could not unhook the lifeless creature from his talons.

Dominick and Dino carefully spread Kelly's claws. Dom put on a funny face, picked up the dead mouse by the tail and dropped it down the sewer—one good hawk meal gone to waste.

"How disgusting!" said Theresa Scalzo.

"When he learns how to catch cockroaches, I'll send him over to your house," smiled Dino.

"You'll be sorry you said that," screamed Theresa as she stomped off to tell her big brother. Cherry Nose Scalzo was tough. He could smoke those smelly, black Italian cigars and never get sick.

"We better disappear," said Dino to Dominick.

"YOU disappear," said Dominick. "YOU said it!"

You don't have to say much to a Scalzo to make him or her angry, and the last thing Dino needed was an angry Cherry Nose on his trail.

Kelly perched on the boy's shoulder as Dino developed a perfect limp—just in case Cherry Nose should suddenly appear. Dino fantasized that maybe he could catch the measles before he got home and be quarantined until he got out of grammar school.

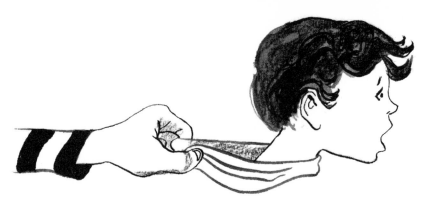

****

Dino was a block and a half from home when Cherry Nose caught up with him.

"Hey, Dino, you're gonna get your face pushed in. Right now!"

"You wouldn't hit a cripple, would you?"

Kelly kept fluttering around Dino's head, and the boy was afraid that the hawk could somehow get hurt. The best thing for Dino to do was to take Scalzo's best punch, hit the deck and stay there—which, of course, is exactly what happened.

Dino's dues came short and sweet. Sitting in the gutter with a swollen lip was the first time, in a long time, that the young bird fancier was at a loss for words. He looked up at Cherry Nose, prepared to give a totally defiant, belligerent Italian apology when he had to burst out laughing.

As Dino had hit the pavement, Kelly had settled on Cherry Nose's curly head and had sunk his talons in his hair. Scalzo was petrified. He was afraid to move a muscle.

"You look like a statue with a pigeon on your head," laughed Dino.

Dino was no dope. He knew that he was only seconds away from being smashed to a pulp.

"Take him off! Take him off!" pleaded the frozen Scalzo.

"On one condition. That you don't lay a hand on me until I'm thirty-seven years old," demanded Dino.

"Twenty-seven, and it's a deal," said Scalzo.

Kelly began to screech and flutter. Cherry Nose was about to pass out with fear when Kelly hopped back on Dino's shoulder. Dino said he was sorry about the roaches—sorry that the Scalzos had them, that is.

There was no such thing as a handshake in this neighborhood. Cherry Nose said he'd settle this when Dino was twenty-seven years old. They parted, backing away from each other, and everything was back to normal.

****

As if the encounter with Cherry Nose was not enough, Dino heard shouts of anger coming from his mother's kitchen. He lingered at the back porch and listened. It was Uncle Pasquale and his mother yelling at each other in their Italian dialect. All Dino had to hear were words like "falconi" and "pigeoni," and it was not hard to figure out what they were yelling about. He might as well go in and face the music and find out what was wrong.

Pasquale glared down at Dino and the hawk. Antonia glared up at Pasquale.

"Two of my young pigeons are dead; their heads are missing," growled Pasquale.

"When did it happen?" asked Dino.

"Today, just a little while ago. Your mother wasa gonna show me the falconi and it wasa gone. Itzza no in your room. Itzza fly over to my pigeon coop and it killed two of my baby pigeons."

Kelly fluttered to the top of Dino's head.

"Look, Uncle Pasquale, Kelly caught a mouse today. He was with me all afternoon. Kestrels don't raid pigeon coops. They catch living things that run and move and fly. Your pigeons are still fledglings and they can't fly, so a cat or a rat ate them—NOT Kelly Anunzio!"

"Whats a fledge-a-ling?" asked Pasquale.

"I dunno," said Dino, "but they can't fly."

"I gotta shotgun, Mr. Smart Guy, and if I see him anywhere near my pigeon coop, I'ma gonna shoot him! Cabeesh?" bellowed Pasquale. "Maybe I'll shoot him right offa you head. Whattza matter with you lip?"

"Cherry Nose tried to kill me."

"Maybe heeza gonna save me the trouble."

Dino knew he meant it. He also knew that Kelly was innocent. How he was going to prove it was another matter.

He took Kelly to his room. There was a commotion in the corner. A mouse squealed as it made a frantic effort to get under Dino's bed as quickly as possible. Kelly lifted himself from Dino's head and hurled himself at the terrified mouse. In a flash it was over. Kelly had decided no more chicken heads for him. He quickly devoured the mouse but looked as though he was not quite sure what he had done.

Dino sat on the edge of the bed, knowing full well what had happened, and contemplated the future. Kelly Anunzio had just become a full-fledged hunter and could now fend for himself. Dino's days with his beloved falcon were numbered.

****

The time had come for Dino to seriously consider giving Kelly his freedom. He was certain the kestrel was not guilty of raiding Uncle Pasquale's pigeon coop—at least, not yet—but he also realized what a stubborn man his uncle was.

There was really only one way to solve the situation. He eventually would have to return Kelly to the Fairfield marshes and expose him to the field mice, shrews and other wild creatures on which he could feed and survive. Catching a city mouse that was cornered in a bedroom was no fantastic accomplishment, but it was a beginning. Although Kelly would have to stay with Dino a few more weeks, Dino would have to resolve this pigeon business right away. Otherwise, Kelly might not survive in this neighborhood.

The next day, Dino locked Kelly in his room. A few doors down the street was Pasquale's tenement. Dino climbed the fire escape to the roof. He heard the soft cooing of the homing pigeons. He checked the haphazard nests that the pigeons had built. "Boy, what sloppy nests," he said to himself.

There were two females setting on their eggs while another nest seemed to have been abandoned. What Dino saw next sickened his heart. There were a beautiful pigeon and her two young squabs lying lifeless in the straw.

For certain, Kelly was innocent. Dino made his way down the fire escape. He must confront Uncle Pasquale and settle this once and for all.

****

The light from the streetlamp filtered through the leaves of the one staghorn sumac tree on the whole city block. It was a warm summer's evening, and most of the kids were playing ring-a-levio or "Buck, buck; How many fingers up?"

The old people sat on their front steps, quietly gossiping in their native dialects. The smell of freshly baked bread came from Altieri's Italian Bake Shop. Some of the kids chipped in and bought a large pizza while others tried to steal a stick of pepperoni from Mamma Ciafoni's Grocery Store. She always caught the culprits and put the cost of the stolen item on their parents' books. Mamma Ciafoni had the whole street on her books. People paid when they had the money or if they won on the daily number.

White-haired Italian men with dark, brown faces were playing bocci, "Throw the big ball after the small ball." Tony, the barber, was watering his tomato plants. He grew them from seeds in five-gallon olive-oil cans. They were left in front of his shop during the day and carefully brought in each night.

Somewhere, someone was singing a rather awful rendition of "O Sole Mio" when an ear-splitting gunshot shattered the pleasantness of the lazy evening. It was naturally assumed that someone had shot the singer, figuring it was justifiable homicide. Within seconds the street was empty.

Dino peered down from the rooftop to a ghostly neighborhood. Uncle Pasquale grinned with satisfaction at a dead rat that was as big as an overgrown zucchini. Knowing how jumpy the neighborhood was about gunshots in the night, Dino wanted to shout that everything was all right. The twirling, yawning blue light of a police car told him otherwise.

As if watching a silent movie, he saw the police questioning the few people who ventured forth. Dino could understand

every gesture, every hand movement, without hearing a word. The police were now surrounded by a curious crowd that was convinced of its innocence. It was pointless for the police to continue questioning when everyone suddenly forgot how to "speaka da English." The cops aimed their light beams down a few alleyways and slowly cruised away.

Dino and Uncle Pasquale descended the shaky fire escape. Pasquale hid the gun and poured himself a glass of wine. The grin was still on his face and he intended to keep it there for a while. Dino went down to Mamma Ciafoni's and bought a lemon ice. He sat under the streetlight, told everyone his story and shared his ice with a stray dog.

Tomorrow Dino was going to take Kelly Anunzio to the marsh. If the hawk caught something to eat, Dino would leave him where he belonged. It was the way it had to be.

The terrible tenor was murdering "Sorrento," but at least it took Dino's mind off Kelly Anunzio.

****

The bus driver pulled over to the side of the road. He strode down the aisle and stared down at Dino.

"What's in that box?" he demanded.

"A transistor radio. I'm listening to a wild animal show," smiled Dino.

"If I hear it once more, you're getting off the bus, understand?"

As soon as the driver went back to the wheel, Dino gave Kelly a chicken head to keep him quiet. The lady across the aisle was shocked and immediately informed the bus driver.

By this time Kelly had escaped from the box and was making friends with the passengers. At least, he thought he was. Most of the people were hiding under their seats and screaming. The bus driver turned quickly around to find out what all the commotion was about, only to see Kelly fly up to his face and land on his head. He went right through a red light. One lady fainted when she saw the bag full of chicken heads strewn all over the floor of the bus. Luckily the doors flew open when the bus came to a sudden stop. Dino quickly stuffed the chicken heads and Kelly into the box and dashed out the door, right into the arms of a very curious policeman.

"Somebody's trying to hijack that bus," he yelled.

The last thing he saw was the cop, with his gun drawn, sneaking up on the bus and hearing all those ladies still screaming about chicken heads and being attacked by a hawk.

Dino was close enough to the marsh to disappear in the reeds and never be seen again.

****

The peace and quiet of the sea felt good as Dino sat, exhausted, after his long trek through the marshes. Gulls crowded the shoreline. Some of them were dropping clams on the rocks to break the shells open. Flocks of golden plovers exploded from the edge of the water only to fly a few yards down the beach to resume their pecking and probing. To add to Dino's mounting sadness, there was a touch of autumn in the air. The scent reminded him of school. It meant the end of a carefree summer. Saddest of all, it meant giving Kelly up to the wilds.

Dino knew from the start that Kelly belonged here in the marsh. Although the kestrel was full grown, he would not get his adult plumage until next spring.

The boy carefully dug a deep hole in the sand and buried the remaining chicken heads. From that moment the hawk would have to hunt for himself.

Kelly fluttered over Dino's head. His voice changed from a shrill baby cry to the sharp sound of a wild creature. Kelly could be fierce. Dino recalled the way he attacked the mouse in his room, but to satisfy himself that Kelly could make it alone, he had to wait around until Kelly was hungry enough to hunt. He

would not leave until the hawk came back with a mouse, a bird
or even a butterfly. Dino would sleep on the beach all night if
necessary.

The sun began descending below the horizon. The sea
became a dead calm. Silent flocks of gulls made their daily
evening flight to their roosting grounds. Twilight sounds
gradually turned into night sounds. Dino heard a foghorn in
the distance. It was the first time he had ever heard a foghorn.
He looked in the direction of the sound and saw the beam of a
lighthouse low on the horizon, making its presence known by
blinking, every fifteen seconds, in Dino's drowsy eyes.

Kelly perched on a piece of driftwood. He tried to nestle in Dino's hair. Dino pushed him away. No more of this, he thought. His eyes got used to the dark and he kept a sleepy watch on the falcon.

The young boy's lids grew heavier and heavier. His last thoughts were about his mother calling the cops again and how peaceful the foghorn sounded as it became softer . . . and softer . . . and s-o-f-t-e-r.

The hawk fluttered down from his perch and nestled on sleeping Dino's chest.

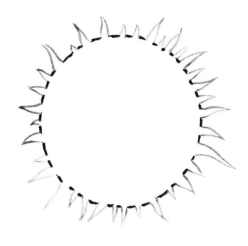

＊＊＊＊＊＊＊＊＊＊＊

Dino awoke with a start. The sun was burning high and bright. Kelly was nowhere in sight. Someone was shouting from the distance. It was too small to be a cop. It wore glasses and had a fake wave in its hair. The closer it got, the more real it looked; and the more real it looked, the more it looked like Dom Dinardo.

"Are the cops looking for me?" asked Dino, flicking the sand from his face.

"Naw, your mother got your note. She sent me to see if you were O.K. and to bring you these salami sandwiches. Pasquale sent you this bottle of wine. Your mother made him cut it with water."

Dino was starved, but he shared his food with Dominick and the gulls.

Dominick decided to explore the beach and once more he became a speck in the distance.

Dino searched the sky for Kelly. He was nowhere to be seen. For Dino, the silence of an empty world had finally fallen upon him. The gulls had left; there were no shorebirds around; Dinardo was gone and so was Kelly Anunzio.

Even the sea was still a dead calm and seemingly motionless. Dino sat and poked holes in the sand and buried his tears where they fell.

****

At first, the sound coming from the sky was hardly noticeable. A slight morning breeze made a hissing sound as it passed through the reeds. The tall grasses bent as the sea began its gentle but stubborn motion to reach the high-water mark.

The soft lapping of the sea water slowly became the sound of crashing waves. The sea had regained its steady rhythm once more, and the sharp sound from the sky seemed to oppose the morning symphony of the Fairfield marshes.

The sound from the sky became much clearer, much closer.

"KLEE . . . KLEE . . . KLEE . . . KLEE . . . KLEE . . . KLEE. . . ."

It was the wild sound of a hunting kestrel. It came from the hungry throat of Kelly Anunzio De Angelo as he screamed above the whistle of the wind and the pounding of the surf.

The falcon hovered high above Dino's head. His wings were trembling in the characteristic way of a kestrel just before making its strike. A flock of sandpipers fled in panic.

The kestrel wheeled in the sky, then suddenly folded its wings and plunged headlong into the reeds. The movement was so wild and beautiful and savage that Dino yelled, "Is that YOU, Kelly Anunzio?" For minutes the falcon was out of sight. Dino could hear him thrashing about in the tall grass. Kelly finally emerged, struggling to keep aloft, as he clung to a squealing field mouse. The little hawk from Lexington Avenue had made his first wild kill!

Kelly returned to the perch beside Dino and spread his long wings over the dead rodent as if to hide it from some prying, sky-bound eye, another characteristic of a bird of prey.

Kelly Anunzio had tasted freedom. The sky, the marsh, the sea, belonged to him and to all wild things. They belonged to the mice that ran in fear from the shadow of a falcon. They belonged to the gulls and the fish crows that rose before the sun. And they belonged to the marsh wrens and blackbirds that sang from the swaying, tufted grass.

The tide rose to where Dino had slept the night. Dino made one last effort to touch Kelly, but Kelly screamed and flew to the dead tree in which he was born.

Kelly could make it now. He was back where he belonged. The tide had risen to the boy's feet, and the teardrops in the sand had become a part of the sea.

It was time for Dino to leave.